Christmas 2018

To KATIE & ELISE & PETER

For being good.

MERRY CHRISTMAS!

From Santa

We Hope You Enjoy Reading!

Kisses & Love,
Aunt Amy
& Aunt Kay
& Aunt Coleen

Santa is coming to Cajun Country

Written by Steve Smallman
Illustrated by Robert Dunn and Katherine Kirkland
Designed by Sarah Allen

Copyright © Hometown World Ltd. 2015

Sourcebooks and the colophon are registered trademarks of Sourcebooks, Inc.

Published by Sourcebooks Jabberwocky, an imprint of Sourcebooks, Inc.
P.O. Box 4410, Naperville, Illinois 60567-4410
(630) 961-3900
Fax: (630) 961-2168
www.jabberwockykids.com

Library of Congress Cataloging-in-Publication data is on file with the publisher.

Source of Production: Leo Paper Products, Guangdong Province, China
Date of Production: May 2015
Run Number: HTW_PO100315
Printed and bound in China
LEO 10 9 8 7 6 5 4 3 2 1

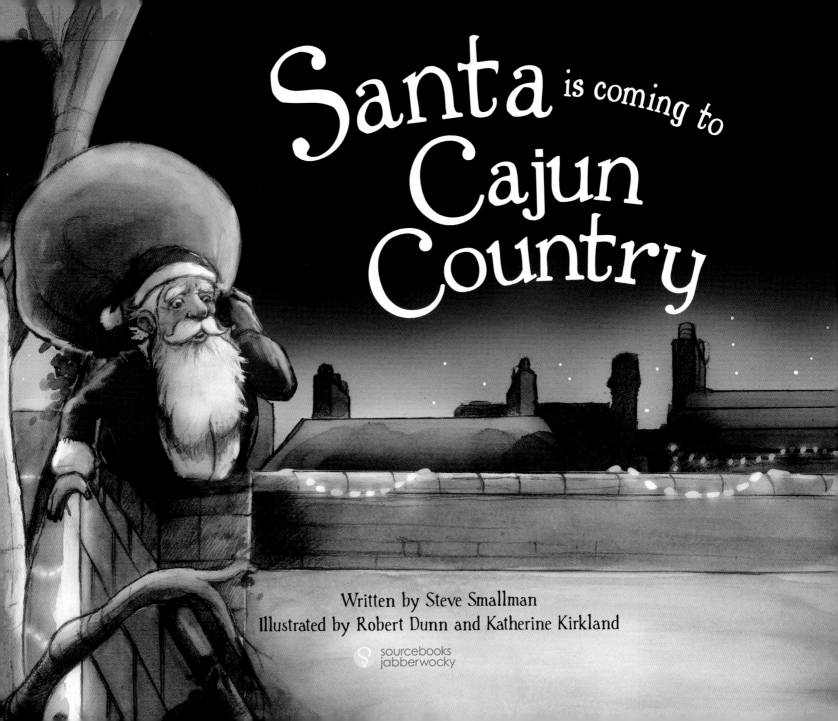

Santa is coming to Cajun Country

Written by Steve Smallman
Illustrated by Robert Dunn and Katherine Kirkland

sourcebooks
jabberwocky

"Well?"

boomed Santa. "Have all the children from **Cajun Country** been good this year?"

"Well...uh...mostly," answered the little old elf, as he bustled across the busy workshop to Santa's desk.

Santa peered down at the elf from behind the tall, teetering piles of letters that the children of Cajun Country had sent him.

"Mostly?" asked Santa,
looking over the top of his glasses.

"Yes...but they've all been **especially** good in the last few days!" said the elf.

"Jolly good!" chuckled Santa.
"Then we'd better get their presents loaded up!"

Even though the sack of presents was

really, really big

and the elves were **really, really** small,

they seemed to have no trouble loading it onto Santa's sleigh.
Though how they managed to fit such a big sack onto one little sleigh
even they didn't know. But somehow they did.

"Splendid!" boomed Santa. "We're ready to go!"

"Er...not quite, Santa," said the little old elf. "One of our reindeer is missing!"

"Missing?

Which reindeer is missing?" asked Santa.

"The youngest one, Santa," said the elf. "It's his first flight tonight. I've called him and called him, but..."

Just then, a young reindeer strolled up, munching on a large carrot.

"Where have you been?"

asked Santa.

But the youngest reindeer was crunching so loudly that it was no wonder he hadn't heard the little old elf calling.

"Oh well, never mind," said Santa, giving the reindeer a little wink.
He took out his Santa-nav and tapped in the coordinates for Cajun Country.
"This will guide us to Cajun Country in no time."

Crunch!
Crunch!
Crunch!

With a flick of the reins and a jerk of the harness, off they went, racing through the sky.

"Ho, ho, ho!"
laughed Santa.

"We'll soon have these presents delivered to Cajun Country!"

Santa's sleigh flew through the starry night, heading south across the Arctic Ocean. On they flew in the wintry air crossing over Canada. In the wink of an eye, the sleigh was flying above Arkansas and past Shreveport. The youngest reindeer was very excited. He had never been away from the North Pole before.

They were flying over Catahoula Lake
when, suddenly, they ran into a thick fog.
Mist swirled around the sleigh.

They couldn't see a thing!

The youngest reindeer was getting a bit worried,
but Santa didn't seem concerned.

"In two miles…"

said the Santa-nav in a bossy lady's voice,

"…keep left at the next star."

"But, ma'am," Santa blustered, "I can't see any stars in all this fog!"
Soon they were

hopelessly lost!

Ding-dong!
Ding-dong!

Then, through the foggy blanket, the youngest reindeer heard a faint ringing sound.

Ding-dong!

He looked over at the old reindeer with the red nose. But he had his head down.

(Red nose...I wonder who that could be?)

Ding-dong!
Ding-dong!
Ding-dong!

Ding-dong!
Ding-dong!

There was that sound again, like church bells ringing. The youngest reindeer turned around to look at Santa. But Santa wasn't listening. He seemed to be arguing with a little box with buttons on it.

With a flick of the harness and a jerk of the reins, the youngest reindeer gave a sharp *tug* and headed off toward the sound of the bells, pulling Santa and his sleigh behind him!

"Whoa!"

cried Santa, pulling his hat straight. "What's going on?" Then, to his surprise, he heard the ringing sound.

"Well done, young reindeer!" he shouted cheerfully. "It must be the bells of the Cathedral of St. John in Lafayette. Don't worry, children, Santa is coming!"

Then, suddenly...

CRUNCH!

The sleigh hit something as it plummeted through the fog.
"You have arrived!"
said the Santa-nav unhelpfully.

Finally, when the fog had lifted, Santa
discovered exactly where they were...

...stuck, right at the very top of the
Christmas tree in
Kemper Williams Park!

"Everybody,
PULL!"

The reindeer *pulled* with all their might until, at last, with a screeching noise, the sleigh scraped clear of the tree. Santa steered them safely over Bayou Teche, above the Evangeline Statue, and down into Jungle Gardens.

Luckily, there was no
real damage done, but
the packages had all been
jumbled up. Santa quickly sorted
the presents into order again.

"All right," said Santa. "Thanks to this
young reindeer I know where we are
now. Don't worry, children,

Santa is coming!"

Santa drove his sleigh expertly from rooftop to rooftop all over Cajun Country, popping in and out of chimneys as fast as he could go. (Which was pretty fast for a chubby fellow!)

There were big chimneys in Lake Charles, and small chimneys in Houma. He squeezed down thin chimneys in Eunice and plummeted down fat chimneys in Lafayette.

The youngest reindeer
was amazed at how quickly
they went. Santa never seemed to
get tired at all! And it looked like
the children in Cajun Country
were going to be very lucky
this year! But the youngest
reindeer was starting to
feel a bit weary and quite
hungry too.

In house after house, Santa delved
inside his sack for packages of
every shape and size.

He piled them under the Christmas trees
and carefully filled up the stockings
with surprises.

Santa took a little bite out of each cookie,
a tiny sip of milk, wiped his beard, and
popped the carrots into his sack.

In house after house, the good children
of Cajun Country had left out a plate of
cookies, a small glass of milk,
and a big, crunchy carrot.

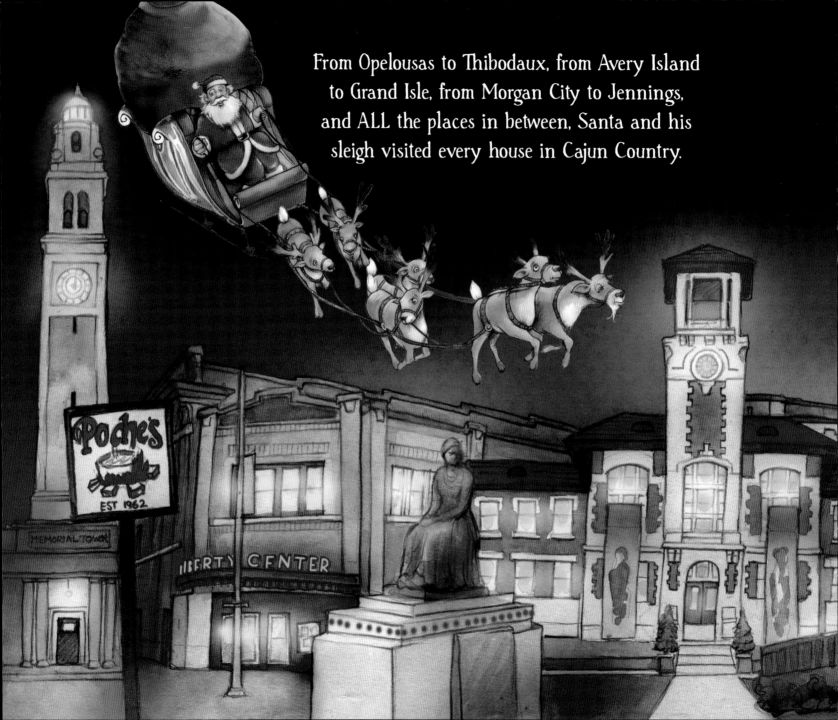

From Opelousas to Thibodaux, from Avery Island to Grand Isle, from Morgan City to Jennings, and ALL the places in between, Santa and his sleigh visited every house in Cajun Country.

Finally, Santa had delivered the last present on his long Cajun Country list.

"Great moons and stars!" sighed Santa. "It's past midnight and my sack seems as heavy as ever! I hope I haven't forgotten anyone."

Santa opened his sack to check...but it was full of juicy, crunchy carrots!

Santa divided the carrots among all the reindeer.
"Well done!" he said, patting the youngest reindeer gently on the nose.

But the youngest reindeer didn't hear him...
he was too busy munching!

Then it was time to set off for home. Santa reset his Santa-nav
once more to the North Pole, and soon they were speeding past
L'Auberge du Lac, above the Cajundome, over Tiger Stadium,
and out through the crisp, starry night.